BOOKI VIVAT

FRAZZLED

EVERYDAY DISASTERS and IMPENDING DOOM

HARPER

An Imprint of HarperCollinsPublishers

Library of Congress Control Number: 2016936039
ISBN 978-0-06-239879-6

Typography by Carla Weise
16 17 18 19 20 CG/RRDH 10 9 8 7 6 5 4 3 2 1

First Edition

To all my readers
who are facing the Middles
in one form or another—
survival is all about
staying true.

CHAPTER ONE

Now that I'm going into middle school, my whole life is about to begin.

That's what Mom told me yesterday. But I didn't know what she meant and I'm pretty sure she didn't either.

Sometimes parents say things because they sound good, even if they aren't true. Like whenever we talk about school, Mom always tells me the same thing over and over again—

—as if saying it will somehow make it more true.

Adults are not helpful at all.

They just don't get it. I guess for most of them, middle school was about a MILLION years ago.

Maybe they forgot all the bad stuff— and there is definitely a LOT of bad stuff.

If you ask me, the worst part about middle school is the fact that it is

MIDDLE SCHOOL.

Nothing good ever happens in the Middles.
Consider:

THE MIDDLE AGES

No electricity, lots of wars, and that whole plague thing.

YIKES!

THE MIDDLE SEAT

ARE WE THERE YET?!?!

Good-bye, personal space.

BEING A MIDDLE CHILD

Trust me. I know from experience— it's TERRIBLE.

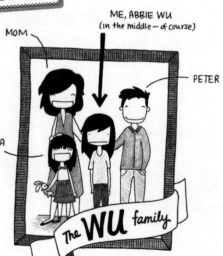

MOM

ME, ABBIE WU
(in the middle—of course)

PETER

CLARA

The WU family

The middle is the worst place you could possibly be, and since middle school is the middle of all Middles . . .

I AM guaRANTeeD WITHOUT-A-DOUBT 100% DOOMED.

I've probably warned everyone I know about the Middles, but no one takes me seriously—not even my own family!

We are NOTHING alike.

Sometimes it feels like we are living in two VERY different worlds.

At the head of the family, there's

Everyone says we look exactly the same, but I don't see the resemblance at all.

Clara is the youngest—fun, bubbly, and annoyingly adorable.

Clara smiles all the time and says cute things at exactly the right moment. Adults LOVE her, so she can pretty much get away with anything.

HOW CREATIVE!

LOOK AT THAT BRUSH TECHNIQUE!

SHE'S LIKE A MINI PICASSO!

She is constantly using this to her advantage.

Peter is the oldest.
He's kind of a legend.
THE Peter Wu—
good at everything,
and I mean EVERYTHING.

Everyone likes him.

My archnemeses,

THE SPENCER SISTERS from next door.

OLD MAN GRIFFIN, treasurer of the homeowners' association and neighborhood snitch.

Even **LUCY**, the demon squirrel that terrorizes Canyon Vista Park.

It's like they are all
part of the same club.

Between Clara
and Peter, I'm
always just that
kid left in the
middle. I guess that's
why I'm keeping a record of my life.

Someday, after I've done lots of ultra-
impressive and exceptional
things, people will look back
and think,

THE ABBIE WU

WOWWW!!! That ABBIE WU was really SOMETHING!

For now, I just have to figure out exactly what
those ultra-impressive, exceptional things will be.

Oh, but first I have to survive middle school and my crazy dreams.

My dream was an obvious sign of things to come, but when I told everybody about it at dinner the other night, they acted like it was no big deal!

Well, except Clara, who was too busy making a mountain out of her rice to pay attention.

RRIBLE!

Peter thought I was being dramatic and Mom just blamed it on late-night snacking.

My family doesn't get me at all.

When we were younger and Peter wanted to be extra mean, he would tell me that I was actually an ALIEN, and one day, they would send me back to outer space.

The first time he said it,
I cried hysterically for an hour.

Mom was so mad that
she grounded him for
a week! It was great.

For the most part, though, Peter never gets into trouble. He practically parents himself.

Clara is starting kindergarten, so there isn't much to worry about there. I guess you can only do so much to prepare a six-year-old for finger painting and naptime.

Mom is so used to not having to worry about them that she doesn't worry about me either! She just isn't a worrier. She always thinks things will work out for the best.

Worrying just doesn't seem to run in the Wu family. Maybe I really AM an alien.

I worry more than anyone I know and maybe more than anyone in the

Now that I'm going into the Middles, how can I not?

CHAPTER TWO

As if to rub in the fact that summer was basically over, I got a package from my new school.

The mailman had to deliver it personally because it didn't even fit in the mailbox.

When he handed it to me, I could've sworn he gave me a look that said:

RUN!

(If only that was an option.)

It was the official Pointdexter Middle School Welcome Packet.

Welcome Welcome Welcome Welcome WELCOME!

But it didn't make me feel welcome at all.

Inside, there were long lists of school supplies and never-ending instructions on how to prepare for class and a million rules and expectations and WAY too much information.

It was more reading than I'd done all summer!

Seeing that welcome packet sent Mom into crazy back-to-school mode. The smell of new  erasers and sharpened pencils must have gotten to her. When we were out shopping, she started prancing down the aisles and gushing over backpacks. Backpacks, of all things!

We left the store with at least three years' worth of wide-ruled paper, every kind of notebook you could possibly imagine, and an assortment of embarrassing cartoon animal folders that I would never ever use in public.

It wasn't just my mom either. When I talked to my best friends, Maxine and Logan, they said their parents were acting really weird too.

Logan's mom made him pose and take pictures in front of the house in his first-day-of-school outfit. The first day of school wasn't even for another week!

Maxine's dad brought out his yearbooks from the seventies and made her look through embarrassing old pictures of him with bell-bottoms and big hair.

I didn't know how any of that was supposed to make us feel better about starting school.

WHAT A FUN ADVENTURE!

MAKE US PROUD!

HOW EXCITING!

ARE YOU READY?

YOU'RE GROWING UP SO FAST!

PARENTS REALLY are CLUELESS.

At least we were in it together. With Maxine and Logan around, the Middles wouldn't be as bad.

The three of us have known each other for a long, long time—since kindergarten, which was basically forever ago.

Kinder Blossom Academy

"The perfect place for your child to grow!"

It all started when Miss Wilson separated us from the class at lunch.

We were forced to sit at a special peanut allergy table for the whole year.

We've been best friends ever since.

Logan Sinclair is the smartest person I know and probably the smartest kid in our grade, but he doesn't care about stuff like that. He thinks class is boring, so he only pays attention when he feels like it. He usually does his homework, but he always forgets to turn it in.

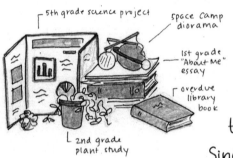

5th grade science project
space camp diorama
1st grade "About Me" essay
overdue library book
2nd grade plant study

I don't understand how his mind works most of the time, but I know for a fact that Logan Sinclair is a GENIUS.

He's the kind of genius that no one knows about until the day he wakes up, decides he wants to take over the world, and then *does it*.

I guess when that happens, being his best friend won't hurt.

Maxine Barry could probably take over the world one day too. She has this amazing superpower: when she wants something to happen, she makes it happen.

Maxine knows everything. According to her, choosing what to wear on the first day of school is the most important thing.

She knows stuff like this because her mom gets her subscriptions to *Seventeen* and *Teen Vogue*. My mom just brings home old copies of *The Economist*.

No wonder I'm

Besides Logan and Maxine, the ONLY good thing about Pointdexter Middle School is that it's right around the corner from my favorite place in the whole world—

You can smell the freshly baked pastries from the school parking lot!

There is no one there named Antonia. I don't think Antonia even exists. The bakery is owned by this old Hungarian man named Istvan who reminds me of a walrus but is nice and doesn't smell like dead fish.

My friends and I go to Antonia's so much that Istvan considers us his "regulars." Plus, if we're there around closing time, he lets us take home as many leftover pastries as we can carry.

Istvan is the best. When I told him I was starting middle school soon, he made a face and just said,

OOF.

He doesn't usually say much, but when he does, he always speaks the truth. Sometimes I think he is the only truly honest adult.

Like one time I wanted a double fudge chocolate chip cookie, but Istvan wrinkled his nose and shook his head a little, so I chose a buttered pretzel covered in homemade cinnamon sugar instead—it was amazing.

31

Not all adults are that honest. On the way home from back-to-school shopping, Mom made a surprise stop at Antonia's and offered to buy me a pastry.

But, turns out, the pastry was a TRAP!

She buttered me up
with baked goods and
then ambushed me
with SCHOOL TALK!

blah blah SCHOOL blah blah blah
blah blah blah
responsibility blah blah blah
ELECTIVES new experiences CHANGE
blah blah blah blah blah blah

Specifically, ELECTIVES.

In middle school, everyone has to choose an
elective class. There are a zillion different
classes to choose from, which sounds like a
good thing but is actually just another trap.

THIS IS DEFINITELY A TRAP.

The worst part is that choosing your elective feels like a declaration, a way of saying to everyone—

That's fine for most people, but I don't HAVE a Thing. I didn't know I needed one until now!

Maxine has known her Thing for years.
She's wanted to be an actress
since third grade.

MISS MILLER'S CLASS
presents...
JAMES AND THE GIANT PEACH

When the boy playing James in
our class play got stage fright,
Maxine swooped in to claim the
lead. No surprise—she
was a hit!

... It's a peach

I, on the other hand, was
cast as Mrs. Ladybug, a
role I conveniently
won by being the

ABBIE WU,
YOUR
LINE!

only kid in class with a red shirt and
a pair of antennae. I wasn't very
good. It was the end of my stage
career, but for Maxine, it was
the moment she found her Thing.
Choosing drama as her elective
was a no-brainer.

36

Even Logan has a Thing. He has always been good at games—so good that he doesn't bother just playing to win anymore. That's not interesting enough.

Instead, he's started figuring out the games themselves, picking them apart and understanding how it all comes together. Card games, board games, strategy games, you name it. Lately, it's been computer games. When he tries to explain them, he uses words that sound like they belong in some distant, high-tech future world. If I didn't know Logan was a genius, I might think he was a

CYBORG.

The second he heard there was a coding elective class that taught you how to program your own computer game, he was sold. I won't be surprised if, by the end of the year, Logan has gained control of the whole internet and all of cyberspace.

School was starting in a few days and I was the only one without an elective!

Logan and Maxine came over to help me choose,
but none of them seemed like a good idea.

We went around in circles for HOURS and couldn't agree on a single one! Luckily, Mom brought out a plate of mini pizza bagels fresh from the oven. Nothing helps you forget your worries like pizza sauce and melted cheese on toasted teeny-tiny bagels.

The truth is, choosing an elective kind of reminded me of the time Mom bought a piñata for my fifth birthday party. People say it's easy because you can cheat and see through the blindfold, but they must be lying because I couldn't see a thing!

FULL OF CANDY AND DELICIOUSLY GOOD STUFF

Everyone just sat there, watching and waiting. Talk about pressure! I stood there swinging and swinging and swinging, but couldn't hit it! They all just laughed until finally one kid jumped up, grabbed the stick, and smashed the piñata open . . . just like that!

MISS!

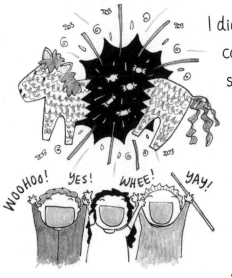

WOOHOO! YES! WHEE! YAY!

I didn't even get any candy because I was still blindfolded!

It was the worst feeling EVER, and facing the Middles without a Thing of my own seemed just as bad.

The night before school started, I couldn't sleep! In a few hours, I would officially be in MIDDLE SCHOOL and there'd be

NO TURNING BACK!

My body was physically refusing to accept it!

Things got even worse when Peter came into my room to tell me I should go to sleep—as if I didn't know that already.

Peter has a way of always getting into my business. He likes to point out things I'm doing wrong or tell me what to do or make me feel crazy.

Sometimes it feels like we will never understand each other. We're just TOO different.

Peter lives in a world where everything always works out for the best.

I live in a constant state of IMPENDIN

That night, all I could think about were the potential disasters waiting for me in middle school.

I bet if Peter had this problem, he wouldn't be able to sleep either.

CHAPTER THREE

I woke up on the first day of school NEAR DEATH.

massive headache

sweaty palms

dry mouth

pounding heart

major stomach aches

shaky legs

Any medical professional would have insisted I stay home, but not Mom.

She dragged me out of bed and told me that I had to be at the bus stop in fifteen minutes . . .

Mom is usually a very relaxed person, but when she gets mad, she morphs into some kind of terrifying

And that morning, she meant business.

I got ready superfast
and caught the bus
right before it left.

PHEW!

Stepping onto the bus was like entering a big,
yellow moving box of chaos. Everyone was
yelling and throwing things across the aisle
and switching seats when the bus driver wasn't
looking. No one bothered with seat belts!

If this was only the ride to middle school, what would actual middle school be like?

Kids on TV always talk about how school is a prison, but I can tell they don't really mean it because the schools on TV look way too fancy to be prisons.

I mean it, though. Pointdexter Middle School really DOES look like a prison.

Building D is the tallest building (four stories!) and all the top windows have thick, metal bars on the outside.

The teachers claim it's for "safety reasons," but Lana Alvarez told me that the whole place used to be a prison in the fifties, but when they decided to change it into a school, all the teachers voted to keep the bars ON.

Lana Alvarez is a HUGE gossip queen
and kind of a troublemaker.

She told me that story right as she was mixing
up the colored caps on Ms. Bennet's whiteboard
markers, so she isn't exactly 100 percent
trustworthy.

point dexter used to be a jail in 1970.
The third seat on bus 41 is haunted.
The the the principal doesn't live on earth.
One Bla only eats the teachers is a vampire.
Ralph only eats Gummy bears are poisonous.
Katrina's mom The teachers lounge is full of candy
The English teacher has a fake nose.
Kara and Zack the nurse steals books from school.
Mr. Gerard broke up Two teachers are dating
Antonia's put has six toes. on his left foot.
Tyler got held back at least twice chocolate tarts.
The new kid got kicked out of 3 schools.

I don't know if it is completely true, but I also
don't know that it's completely UNtrue.

One thing I know for sure: middle school is a LOT bigger than elementary school.

The hallways are bigger!
The buildings are bigger! Even the kids are bigger! I thought I was going to be crushed before I even made it to my first class.

WELCOME!
Attention new students — please head to the main auditorium for your orientation.

The woman standing by the front gate looked too nice to be a teacher. Maybe she worked in the office. I considered asking her how to get to the auditorium, but Maxine told me one rule of surviving middle school was to make sure not to get too chummy with the adults. So I kept walking and figured I'd find it eventually.

When the bell rang, everyone in the auditorium scrambled for a place to sit. I accidentally hit a boy in the face on the way to my seat! It's true what they say about middle school being rough.

Once everyone was settled, a woman in a frumpy suit walked up to the podium and introduced herself. Mrs. Kline looked nice,

but she also looked really tired, kind of like the "before" version of ladies on those makeover shows or like one of those grown-ups who always complains about needing coffee.

I felt a little bad for her, so I tried to pay attention, but everything she was saying was just so

No offense to Mrs. Kline but I had bigger problem to solve . . .

My best friends were in the same homeroom class while I was probably trapped with a bunch of weirdos and jerks I didn't know.

Every one of my teachers was going to see my name during roll call and secretly hope I was a miniature Peter Wu.

WU?

The snotty kid sitting next to me had completely taken over my armrest and smelled like wet cabbage.

57

Then, all of a sudden, Mrs. Kline got this strange look on her face and said:

I look at you & I see so much
POTENTIAL!

NOW is the time to start thinking about your

FUTURE!

What did that even mean? Wasn't it hard enough just to BE in middle school?

By the time I walked into my homeroom class, one of my major middle school fears had already come true.

I had the WORST homeroom teacher in the whole school!

Ms. Skelter

She looked like some kind of evil sorceress with her baggy black dresses and her creepy, bony hands. Some boys in class even started calling her

SKELETOR

Rumor has it, she is actually a MILLION years old, and the only thing keeping her alive are the souls of all the students she hates, which she keeps in the amulet necklace around her neck. She NEVER takes it off.

I'm convinced she has a third eye in the back of her head. When she wasn't looking, Tyler Pritchett started to throw a paper airplane at Hayley Parks, but Skeletor gave him detention before he even let it go!

Talk about scary.

Homeroom was only fifteen minutes long, but it felt like an *eternity*

dontlookupdontlookupdontlookupdontlook

I stared at my empty notebook the whole time because I was afraid if I looked up, I'd make eye contact with Skeletor and get cursed.

It was only my first day of school—I couldn't afford to get cursed.

The bell rang and I was almost out the door, when . . .

Skeletor appeared out of thin air and began to interrogate me.

WHAT'S YOUR NAME?

ABBIE WU...

Then she asked it, the question I had been dreading:

Aren't you related to PETER WU?

When I said no, Ms. Skelter's lip twitched like she KNEW. *I don't know why I decided to lie.*

Maybe it was because I didn't want her to think I was just like him or maybe I was just sick of always being the Middle Wu.

WHO KNEW?

If watching movies should have taught me anything, it was that you did NOT lie to scary underworld creatures who were blocking your escape route.

Somehow I managed to slip past her before she could say anything. I was safe . . .

FOR NOW.

CHAPTER FOUR

The good thing about starting the day with Ms. Skelter is that, by comparison, the other teachers don't seem so bad—at least not YET.

Teachers always pretended to be extra nice in the beginning of the year to catch you off guard.

One thing I know for sure:

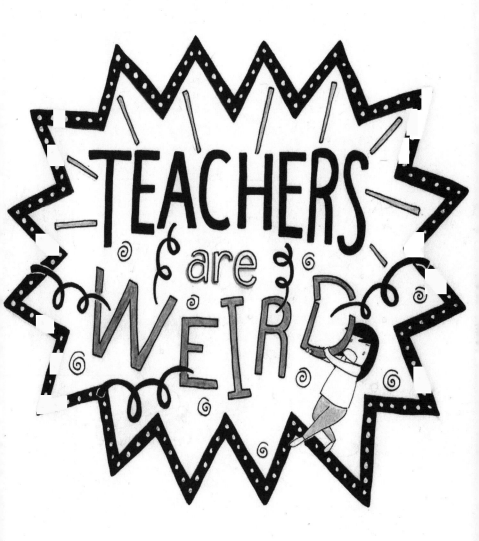

POINTDEXTER MIDDLE SCHOOL'S
FACULTY & STAFF
"We're here for YOU!"

PHOTO NOT AVAILABLE

PRINCIPAL DEWITT
Rarely seen in public.
Rumored to HATE kids.
Might not exist <u>AT ALL</u>.

VICE PRINCIPAL KLINE
Always tired. Makes awkward morning announcements.

MRS. LOPEZ
(THE LIBRARIAN)
Knows books. Nice enough, but OBSESSED with hippos.
WHY HIPPOS?!?!

MR. WALTERS
(THE SCIENCE TEACHER)

Tells corny jokes. Likes science puns. WAY too happy for a teacher. Possibly insane?

MRS. FIELDING
(THE ENGLISH TEACHER)

SUPER quiet. Voice like a mouse whispering through rusted telephone wire.

MR. MONROE
(THE HISTORY TEACHER)

Former member of off-Broadway (WAY off) drama company. Uses class as an excuse to preview theatrical pieces...

MISS MYERS
(THE PE TEACHER)

Secretly dating the 8th grade Spanish teacher, Mr. Prentice. Takes out relationship frustrations on students. YIKES.

Teachers here are completely unpredictable.
Take Miss Myers, for example. Whenever she's
in a bad mood, she makes the whole class
stay late for absolutely NO reason. That is the
worst because, for me, PE is right before lunch!

When I get hungry, two things usually happen:

1. I transform into an unstoppable angry beast.

2. I go crazy.

Sometimes if I stare at the clock for too long, I start thinking about all the lunch foods and wonder whether or not they are as excited about lunchtime as I am. Probably not.

This is probably a sign that I am losing my mind and if I don't get something to eat soon, I will go full-blown crazy starve, and die.

School lunch has always been a tricky business.

EW.

GROSS.

In elementary school, you had to eat the food your parents packed or settle for whatever they served in the cafeteria—the same old rubbery pizza squares or lumpy mashed potatoes or soggy sandwiches every single week.

Kindergarten was worse. They passed out packs of carrot sticks and celery and called them "snacks." That's when I realized that adults have a very warped definition of the word "snack."

In middle school, it was SUPPOSED to get better.

I was actually looking forward to lunch. I had been dreaming about middle school lunches for years, ever since I heard that Pointdexter's cafeteria had REAL food—cheese pizza, burgers and fries, chicken nuggets with BBQ sauce.

There were even rumors of a special snack window that sold all kinds of candies and chips and cookies!

Finally, we'd be able to eat whatever we wanted—cupcakes and curly fries and soda for lunch!

OR SO I THOUGHT.

UGH.

GO AWAY,
LOSERS.

Before I could even get in line, my mortal enemies appeared— the awful, terrible, practically evil Spencer sisters. "Practically evil" because when I said they were FULLY evil, Mom got mad and told me I was exaggerating.

Maybe she was right. But then again, Mom's not the one who had to pull Katie Spencer's chewed bubble gum out of her hair or wrestle her left shoe from Meghan Spencer's clutches.

I am pretty sure their sole mission in life is to make my life miserable—starting with lunch.

Apparently there is a special lunch line for

Now that the Spencer sisters are in eighth grade, they are determined to make sure we NEVER use it.

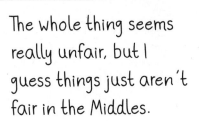

The whole thing seems really unfair, but I guess things just aren't fair in the Middles.

The line for everyone else is all the way on the opposite side of the cafeteria.

It's so long that it wraps around the entire quad. By the time we found the end and got in line, it was all the way past the trash cans!

I caught a whiff of uneaten tuna sandwiches, Funyuns, and pepperoni pizza soaked in a weird soda-juice mixture.

GROSS.

We finally made it to the front of
the line. I stepped up to the cafeteria
window expecting this:

freshly cut flowers

homemade cupcake with extra frosting

folded cloth napkin and real silverware

ABBIE

Soda in a fancy glass (w/ lemon)

fresh french fries with multiple dip options

ripe fruits (no seeds)

juicy cheeseburger

Instead, all they seemed to have was this:

soggy vegetable mix

sink water in a foam disposable cup

stale bread roll

rubbery pieces of mystery meat

plastic spork and knife

bland mush with brown gravy sauce

There had to be a mistake!

When I tried to ask for something else, this mean, ogre-ish-looking cafeteria lady just stared at me from behind the counter. She growled like she wanted to rip off my head with her stubby claws and said,

YOU CAN'T ORDER THAT HERE.

Turns out, all the food we want is sold at the eighth-grade cafeteria window—the one we aren't allowed to use!

I couldn't believe it!
Nothing made sense in middle school!

CHAPTER FIVE

As if the lunch situation wasn't bad enough, because I didn't choose an elective, they stuck me in the worst one—

STUDY HALL.

Study hall isn't a REAL class.
It doesn't even have a real classroom!

To get there, you have to walk all the way past the science building and across the soccer field to this cluster of

junky, beat-up TRAILERS!

The school tries to make it sound all official by calling it a "temporary annex wing of portable classrooms," but everyone knows what it REALLY is—an exiled wasteland of classes no one actually cares about.

And of course, study hall is the farthest away.

Study hall doesn't have a REAL teacher either. I heard the old one had a mental breakdown last year and got shipped off to a psych ward. And because I am the unluckiest person in the world and the Universe hates me, the school put Ms. Skelter in charge!

Some people think Skeletor hexed the old teacher so she could take over the class and use its students as guinea pigs in her twisted, evil experiments. I don't doubt it.

MWAHAHAHAHAHAHAHAHAHA

The other thing about study hall is that there is no purpose for it. The class description says it is:

An elective course designed to improve study skills, supplement academic instruction, and promote independent activity.

That is basically school talk for

The RULES of STUDY HALL

#1 SHOW UP

Abbie Wu...?

I'M HERE!!!

#2 STAY AWAKE

#3 STUDY

concentrate...
concentrate...

And even then, the last two are pretty optional.

Maxine says that the key to surviving class is to find friends and allies, but I don't think I want to be allies with anyone in study hall—let alone friends!

82

The kind of people who purposefully choose study hall as an elective are:

SUCK-UPS

who legitimately want to spend the whole time studying (ugh)

SLACKERS

Who just want a free period to sleep or stare at the wall

TROUBLE-MAKERS

who like the idea of trouble without ever getting into it

LONERS

who don't have friends or interests and don't care about anyone or anything at all

. . . and now **ME**

Does that make me one of THEM?

It was only the beginning
of the year, and I had
already:

Lied to at least three
teachers.

Been blacklisted by the
cafeteria staff.

Swallowed
an eraser
(well, ALMOST
swallowed) in a fit
of blind hunger.

Somehow my life was already a

When it came down to it,
I blamed the Middles.
I blamed middle school.

The way I saw it, school was like this
GIGANTIC BLACK HOLE.

It was a weird place.
Time stood still.

Everything was confusing
and mixed-up and
NOTHING made
sense

—at least not to me.

I called an EMERGENCY BEST FRIEND
MEETING for after
school, then spent
all of study hall
brainstorming
alternative
non-school-related
lifestyle options for us:

1. Run away and join
the circus. Maybe this
wasn't the best idea
since we'd probably end
up having to ride in that
crowded clown car.

2. Become
international pop
stars. They didn't
have to go to
school, right?

3. Time travel to the future, where school is irrelevant and all knowledge can be downloaded into your head by swallowing a microchip.

I didn't get a chance to share my ideas with them because the minute Maxine, Logan, and I started talking about school, I found out . . .

THEY *liked* **IT.**

How was that even possible?
Were we even going to the same school??
Were we even living in the same dimension???

It got worse when Maxine and Logan started talking about how GREAT their electives were and how much FUN they were having.

Everyone sucks. What's going on? argh

? This is too hard. ✗ ugh !

E e blah ! meh !

? Middle school is the worst. ?

ew ✗

I couldn't take it! It was all they wanted to talk about!

Ever since we started at Pointdexter, things had been a little *off*. The Middles had a way of making me feel like I was always being left behind.

Maxine finally had the chance to live out her acting dreams, and Logan found a constructive outlet for his weird genius mind powers. It wouldn't be long before things started taking off from there.

It felt like their lives were getting further and further away from mine.

But we were BEST FRIENDS. That wasn't supposed to happen!

MIDDLE SCHOOL *was* Changing EVERYTHING.

CHAPTER SIX

Well, maybe not EVERYTHING was changing. At home, things were more or less the same.

Peter was still the star player of the high school soccer team.

Clara was still as cute and conniving as ever. Apparently now she was also a budding artist and she made sure to rub it in my face every time I wanted a snack.

THIS IS
ART.
NO
TOUCHING.

Mom still seemed to think middle school was an "exciting new adventure," even though it was very obviously NOT.

My weekly routine hadn't changed much either.

MONDAY:
Definitely still
the hardest
morning of
the week.

TUESDAY: My regular
after-school visit to
Antonia's. Istvan DID
add a new double
fudge chocolate cake
to the selection, but
THAT was a change I could handle.

WEDNESDAY: *Wheel of Fortune* marathon with
the family—even though it was totally unfair
that you could lose everything just because
the spinner landed on

BANKRUPT.
NOOOOOOO.....

THURSDAY: Laundry day.

FRIDAY: Family dinner with Aunt Lisa. After dinner, she and Mom always watched *Law & Order* and fell asleep within twenty minutes. I don't think they ever finished an episode . . .

and she had been coming over for as long as I could remember! At this point, it was basically a Wu family tradition.

I used to think this kind of stuff made us boring, but ever since the Middles started turning my life upside down, I didn't mind so much. There were enough things changing in my life, thank you very much.

Plus, I like Aunt Lisa. She is an older, tanner version of Mom— only way kookier. Everyone thinks she's nuts.

Well, Mom calls her a "free spirit."

Aunt Lisa lives in a mobile home because she likes the idea of being able to pick up her life and go somewhere new—even though it has been parked in the same exact spot for years.

I am almost positive it isn't really "mobile" anymore.

Aunt Lisa is very into karma and cosmic energy and something called "hot yoga." She is always saying strange things. In the middle of dinner, she suddenly stopped eating and declared:

I sense there's an *imbalance* in the Universe!

I don't know why she looked at ME.

If the Universe was imbalanced, it wasn't MY fault...

 Could it be because I didn't have a Thing? Could I really be the ONLY ONE left in the Universe without a Thing?

I always thought the Universe was supposed to send me some kind of sign. Like, all of a sudden, I would discover that I was a genius at something and that would be my sign from the Universe and THAT would be my Thing.

But so far . . . NOTHING.

I hoped that the Universe would get back on track by the end of dinner, but then Aunt Lisa cornered me in the kitchen and asked:

HOW IS your CORE?

I didn't even know I HAD a core. How was I supposed to know if it was okay?

Usually when adults ask about your life, they want you to spill your guts and tell them everything so they can be "involved."

Aunt Lisa doesn't REALLY count, though. She isn't your "typical adult," the kind that always complains about taxes or insurance claims or real estate.

If I was going to talk to anyone about my problems, Aunt Lisa was my best bet.

Still, I wasn't always sure I trusted her advice. It usually had something to do with meditating.

The Wus are NOT made for meditation. Mom usually falls asleep halfway through, and I clearly can't do it right because both my legs always go numb.

um...
Aunt Lisa
...Help?

I CAN'T FEEL MY LEGS OMG I'M GOING TO DIE WHAT IS GOING ON MEDITATING IS THE WORST

Peter is the only one who looks like he's actually meditating, but then one day, I found out that he secretly listens to music the whole time. When I confronted him about it, he just shrugged and said:

Sometimes it's **better** to do what works for **you**.

Meditation might not be our thing, but it seems to work for Aunt Lisa. She says listening is a part of meditating, and she is a VERY good listener.

When I finished telling her everything, she closed her eyes and was quiet for a long time. I thought she might have fallen asleep.

Then, all of a sudden, she opened her eyes and said:

Sometimes, IF you STOP THINKING so much, things just FIGURE themselves OUT.

Stop thinking? That seemed impossible. Even so, I felt better after talking to her. It might have helped that she also treated me to ice cream later.

Best advice EVER!

The funny thing is, I DID stop thinking about it after a while . . . but only because I had

Between the group projects, dioramas, book reports, work sheets, essays, write-ups, presentations, tests, quizzes, homework, and reading assignments, there just wasn't TIME to think about anything else! I got a huge headache just THINKING about thinking.

Learning is FUN!!!

It didn't look like lunch was EVER going to get better. I knew there would be bullies in school, but I didn't expect them to be wearing hairnets and serving food.

The whole cafeteria system was completely corrupt and the lunch ladies were basically heartless.

They expected us to wait for food that wasn't even real food. Worst of all, the eighth-grade line was right there torturing us! We could see and smell everything we weren't allowed to have!

PIZZA.
BURGERS.
FRENCH FRIES.
NUGGETS.

You name it.

One time, we tried to pass as eighth graders, but the Spencer sisters were patrolling the line like hawks. They kicked us out before we could even get to the cafeteria window.

I thought lunch would be better in middle school; it was only better if you were in eighth grade, and that was a whole TWO YEARS away.

Once again, Mom's packed lunch was my only option. But when I opened my lunch box, it was worse than I could've ever imagined:

The whole thing was a disaster waiting to happen.

If I opened the Tupperware, the whole cafeteria
would start to smell . . .

. . . and just like that,
my middle school social life
would be OVER.

I could NOT let
that happen.

Of course, the Spencer sisters showed up at our table with huge slices of extra-cheesy pizza just to rub it in our faces. I tried to pretend like I wasn't jealous, but the drooling gave me away.

I hadn't eaten anything since breakfast, and that didn't really count. I was the last one to the table, so I got stuck with the cereal crumbs at the bottom of the box. Typical.

Halfway through study hall, it really started to hit me. I could feel my hunger building. It was grumbling and rumbling and growing until I just couldn't control it anymore!

Then the unspeakable happened. Mu stomach made the

The classroom went dead silent for a second. That's when I knew that EVERYONE had heard it.

They ALL knew it was ME—

?

HOW EMBARRASSING!

I could feel them looking. I could hear them whispering. For the rest of the year, I'd be THAT girl—the girl who made weird noises in class. The GRUMBLER.

I couldn't live like that.

Good thing I always had an escape plan handy.

But then, in the middle of plotting my new identity and ironing out the details of my life on the run, I heard a rumble even louder than mine!

I turned around to see Mikey Mathers grabbing HIS stomach. I thought he would cry from the embarrassment, but instead, he looked right at me and smiled. Then he started laughing his head off!

I always suspected he was crazy. Now I knew for sure.

Maybe I was a little crazy too. Before I knew it, I was laughing WITH him.

Then everybody in class started laughing—
TOGETHER.

We didn't stop until Ms. Skelter shushed us
and threatened to give us all detention.

After that day, things just felt DIFFERENT.

Something about knowing we were all kind of, sort of in this thing together made it a little more bearable.

We talked a lot about how unfair it was that eighth graders got a special lunch line and how we were always SO hungry after lunch was over.

This was when I learned that everyone has something they just don't like in their lunch box.

One day, I was complaining about having cherry-grape fruit rolls for lunch AGAIN.

I always left them uneaten in my lunch box hoping that Mom would get the hint, but she never did. First off, cherry and grape are two of the worst fruit flavors.

They're bad enough on their own, but TOGETHER?

NO THANKS.

Secondly, there are four different flavors in a box of twenty-four— strawberry-melon, cherry-grape, lime-orange, and mixed berry.

NOW IN FOUR delicious FRUIT FLAVOR COMBINATIONS!

Smacker's FRUIT ROLLS

KID APPROVED

Mom packs them randomly, but honestly, what are the odds of getting cherry-grape FOUR days in a row?

Cherry-grape. EW.

WHAT? AGAIN?

Seriously? This HAS to be a CONSPIRACY.

HOW IS THIS EVEN POSSIBLE?

I bet Peter and Clara NEVER got cherry-grape.

That day in study hall, I found out that Mikey
LOVED cherry-grape. He offered to trade
me his whole bag of peanut butter-covered
pretzels for
them, but I was
allergic and if
I ate one, I'd
probably blow
up like a balloon
and he'd get in trouble
for poisoning me.

yum! My favorite!

Amy Becks overheard us talking and she
really wanted those pretzels . . . so much so
that she was willing to give up a
whole bag of cheese puffs! That
seemed crazy to me because
I thought cheese puffs
were delicious, but
Amy said she thought
it was gross that they
turned her fingers
and tongue orange.

CHEESE PUFFS

It got me thinking. A little organized switching and we could each get exactly what we wanted.

THAT was how it all began.

At first, it was just a couple of us swapping snacks in the back of the classroom. Our study hall trailer was pretty small, though, and before long, more people wanted in.

So here's what we do...

Then things started getting tricky.

Eventually, Ms. Skelter took notice and asked what we were doing. I blurted out,

It's a... group project for Mr. Monroe's class!

One look at the spread of lunch leftovers on the table and her eyes narrowed. I thought for SURE we were caught.

Then, out of nowhere,
Alexis Bunker
popped up behind us
and said matter-of-factly—

Our group is doing a modern-day study of the importance of bartering and economic exchanges.

I almost fell out of my seat—
I couldn't believe it!

I wasn't the only one either. Edgar Ortiz's jaw looked like it was about to detach from the rest of his face and Ellen Smith's eyes were just about ready to pop out of her head.

This was Alexis Bunker. If you looked up "teacher's pet" in a dictionary, she'd be right there at the very top.

She was one of those people who joined study hall because she legitimately wanted to study. I had never seen her talk in class without raising her hand, and I had DEFINITELY never seen her lie to a teacher. Maybe that's why they all trusted her.

Ms. Skelter totally bought it. I guess even Alexis Bunker knew that we were in this together now. Later on, she dropped a package of rice cakes on the table and asked if I could help her get something in exchange.

RICE CAKES?
Basically Styrofoam.

It was a tough sell, but eventually, I made a deal and traded the rice cakes for Fritos. Alexis was SO happy.

I have NEVER seen someone eat a whole bag of chips that quickly. I guess it makes sense, though. I mean, seriously, what kind of parent packs their kid rice cakes for lunch?

CHAPTER EIGHT

I didn't know it at the time, but that was only the beginning.

After school, I went to the playground with Logan and Maxine, only we weren't supposed to call it "the playground."

Once you're in middle school, you can't "play" anymore—you have to "hang out."

Anyway, that's when I told them everything!

They couldn't believe it—

...AND THEN SHE **LIED** TO SKELETOR!

WHAAAT?!?

NO WAY.

Especially the part about swapping snacks right under Skeletor's nose!

Logan gave me a high five and
Maxine said:

THAT IS SO amazing!

"Sounds like you're the one in charge of study
hall now! You're like their leader!"

I hadn't thought about it that way.

Did I somehow become the
leader of our small,
unofficial cafeteria
rebellion?

Me?

133

"Cool. You're kind of like . . . the Godfather of snacks."

"You're queen of the lunch swap!"

Maybe that was a bit much, but I didn't completely hate the way it sounded.

After all, I was NEVER the mastermind.

Logan was the smart one and Maxine had all the creativity, which usually just left me somewhere in the middle. I didn't mind most of the time, but once in a while, it was nice to be the one with the good idea.

We spent the rest of the day imagining all the things I could do if I was REALLY queen.

The thought of our enemies as court jesters and pig farmers and onion peelers made us laugh so hard I thought our stomachs would explode!

Pointdexter Middle School was not a monarchy, and even if it was, I definitely wasn't its queen . . . but at the same time, I knew what the people wanted.

When it came to lunch, we ALL wanted something different than what we had. That's when it hit me—

Things at school weren't going to change anytime soon. Eighth graders had the cafeteria ladies under their control, and that didn't leave the rest of us with many options.

Unless...

What if we came up with something that no one at this school had ever thought of before?

It sounded a little crazy, but it was EXACTLY what we needed.

Who knew?

This could be a Thing.

THIS COULD BE
MY
THING

Then it wouldn't matter that the Spencer sisters
stopped us from using the eighth-grade-only
line. It wouldn't matter that there was an
eighth-grade-only line at all!

The cafeteria ladies might still be mean and our parents might still be clueless about snacks, but maybe if we worked together, everyone could get what they wanted.

LET'S DO IT!

Now that I had my team assembled, our first step was to figure out a plan, and for that, we needed . . .

Actually, we needed to THINK, but the two were sort of related.

We decided to meet at Antonia's Bake Shop after school every day that week. It became our official headquarters.

Istvan let us stay as long as we needed to—
or at least until closing time.

Plus, he had this magical ability of knowing
exactly what we wanted without even having
to ask.

We did our best work at Antonia's.

To pull off something this big, we would need more help. Luckily, everyone was pretty sick of the cafeteria rules.

First order of business: Recruit Lana Alvarez, Pointdexter gossip queen, to spread the word.

By fourth period, not only did everyone know that something was going on, they all wanted to be a part of it!

Meanwhile, Logan put all the kids in his coding class to work on mapping out a digital tracking system of delivery and exchange sites.

I didn't fully understand what they were doing. Something about programming a virtual layout of the school into everyone's phone. It sounded complicated, but if anyone could get it to work it was Logan.

I could always count on him to figure out the confusing stuff.

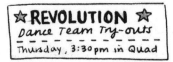

Maxine was a "people person," so she got her friends on Student Council to sneak hidden messages into the flyers around school and used her texting expertise to create an elaborate communication system made up of only emojis.

Within a week or so, our little lunch exchange had spread beyond just study hall and made its way across the entire school campus.

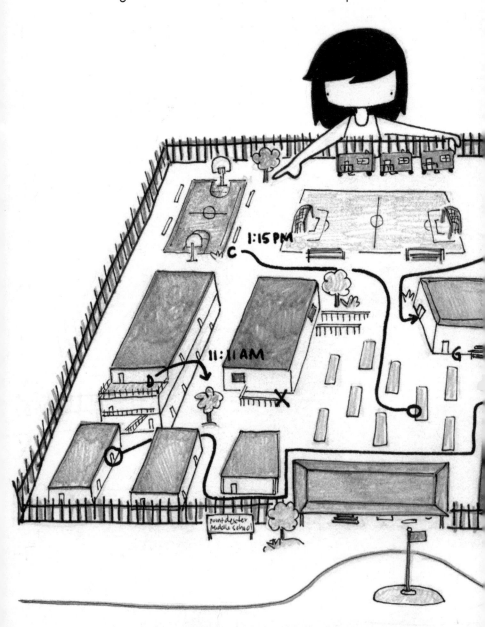

Pointdexter Middle School was changing,
and we weren't just a part of that change—
we were the ones changing it.

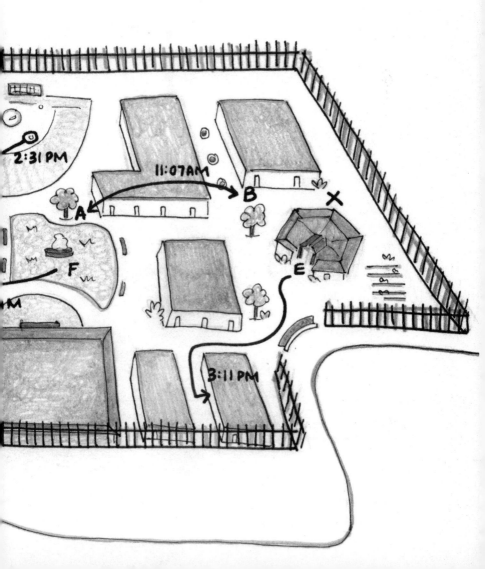

After a while, the teachers and lunch ladies started to notice a major drop in the regular cafeteria line, but no one knew why.

Except US, of course.

Things were changing for me too. I didn't know if the Middles were getting easier or if I was just getting used to them, but I wasn't about to question it.

Everyone was talking about the lunch exchange.

They were right too. Everything WAS different.

Not too long ago, the only seats we could get were at the sad, defective lunch table on the far end of the quad.

The tabletop was faded and crusty from old bits of food. The bench was covered in a sticky, permanent layer of leftover juice or soda. We had to sit on sheets of notebook paper just so our pants wouldn't get stained!

Finding a table at lunch used to be impossible, but now we ALWAYS had one.

It was like we FINALLY made it.

Now people actually knew who we were—
who *I* was!

I was more than just Peter's sister or the
unexceptional middle Wu. Without even fully
realizing it, I had become the center of this
whole lunch revolution.

It was my
THING.

The bigger the lunch exchange got, the more it became something beyond just us. Someone started calling it

POINTDEXTER's lunch REVOLUTION

and the name just stuck. News of it had even reached the high school!

POINTDEXTER MIDDLE SCHOOL

HAMILT
HIGH SC

I tagged along with Peter to the movies one night, and while we were waiting for the movie to begin, his friends started talking about OUR lunch exchange. They even asked me if I knew about it!

I shrugged and pretended like I didn't know ANYTHING.

Even though I found my Thing, I still felt off about it. How could I be so UNSURE of something I was so SURE about? Maybe there was something wrong with me, something I wasn't doing right. When you found your Thing, nothing could go wrong . . .

That was how it worked.

So why did I still have this feeling that I was on the brink of disaster? Maxine and Logan kept saying there was nothing to worry about, but I couldn't help thinking that things were coming to an end.

CHAPTER NINE

Turns out, I was RIGHT. It had been a perfectly normal day until a huge, dark cloud started hovering over the classroom trailer.

FORESHADOWING?

When I walked into study hall, things were definitely off.

Everyone was huddled in the back of the room around Alexis Bunker, who was completely

When she saw me, she made this wailing noise and started mumbling hysterically—

I should have known what was coming next.

It was one of those moments where you're watching things happen, but you never fully realize it is happening to YOU until it's too late.

It was like I was in a movie theater watching my own personal middle school drama play out before me onscreen. . . .

FADE IN.

Suddenly there are heavy footsteps outside the classroom and a knock on the door.

Enter a snooty-faced office aide. She hands Ms. Skelter a bright-pink note.

They both glance up and look straight at **ME** . . .

[cue dramatic music]

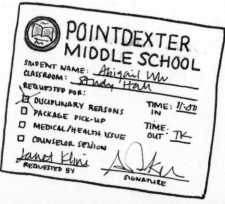

"Take your bags" meant you weren't just visiting the office. "Take your bags" wasn't just a little bit of trouble. "Take your bags" was the nail in the coffin. "Take your bags" was the worst-case, end-of-the-line, doomsday scenario.

The journey across the school felt a million times longer than it normally did. I could feel a million eyes following my walk of shame all the way up to the front office.

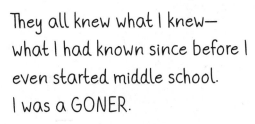

They all knew what I knew—
what I had known since before I
even started middle school.
I was a GONER.

CHAPTER TEN

The vice principal called me into her office and looked disapprovingly at me from behind her desk. I had never been in Mrs. Kline's office before. It smelled a lot like dust and burnt toast.

I had never *talked* to Mrs. Kline either, and to be honest, I had never wanted to. She seemed like she meant business—especially now. After all, she started out by calling me:

MISS WU...

Maxine has a theory that whenever an adult calls you by your last name, it means you are in serious trouble—that or they can't remember your first name.

This was probably the first time in my entire life that I actually WANTED someone to forget my name, but by the look on Mrs. Kline's face, I knew that wasn't it.

After a while, it started to hit me. Sweaty palms, shaky knees, the undeniable urge to bite my fingernails—all surefire signs that I was about to crack under pressure.

WHAT DO YOU KNOW ABOUT THIS LUNCH EXCHANGE? I HOPE YOU REALIZE THIS IS A SERIOUS MATTER. SO WERE YOU OR WERE YOU NOT INVOLVED?

Mrs. Kline must've been a CIA interrogator in her past life.

I tried to channel Clara, who always had a knack for getting out of trouble. I clearly didn't share my little sister's acting talents. Despite my best attempts to look simultaneously innocent and clueless, it didn't seem to work.

Then a voice came in through the intercom:

I have **MRS. BUNKER** for you on line one...

it's about our *LUNCH SITUATION* — and it sounds...

IMPORTANT.

MRS. BUNKER—just hearing the name gave me chills.

Alexis Bunker's mother was notoriously scary.

Mrs. Bunker was one of the parent chaperones on our first-grade class field trip to the zoo. She made her group hold hands the ENTIRE time and wouldn't give them their snack packs until they recited at least five CORRECT animal facts.

Even worse, she made Alexis wear a harness. I'm not even sure it was a *kid* harness—it looked more like an old dog leash to me.

Mrs. Bunker HAD to be in control. If she somehow found out about our secret lunch exchange, there would be SERIOUS consequences.

Apparently the trouble started when she found cheese stains on Alexis's homework packet. The dietary regimen in the Bunker house is very strict and does NOT include cheese puffs.

Cheese prints EVERYWHERE!

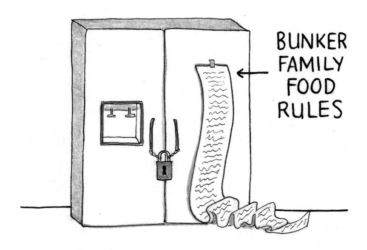

BUNKER FAMILY FOOD RULES

And I thought MY mom was tough because she wouldn't let us have cereal with marshmallows for breakfast! If I was a Bunker, I would definitely starve.

I think Mrs. Bunker trained their family dog to sniff out artificial flavoring, which is probably how she found the empty bag of cheese puffs crumpled at the bottom of Alexis's backpack.

IS that PROCESSED CHEESE?

Alexis was caught red-handed . . . or whatever the cheese puff equivalent of that would be.

Her mom threatened to send her to boarding school in Switzerland if she didn't confess everything. Most parents just said that without meaning it, but Mrs. Bunker never made empty threats.

cheese fingers

So Alexis told her mom and her mom told the school and that was it—our whole operation brought down by cheese puffs!

Maybe this was what people meant when they said junk food was bad for you.

When Mrs. Kline asked me to wait outside her office while she talked to Mrs. Bunker, I knew it was REALLY bad for me.

I hated getting in trouble, but I hated WAITING to get in trouble even more. Next to the Middles, waiting was the WORST.

You were stuck in between something that had already happened and something that was going to happen—right in the middle where NOTHING was happening.

Waiting for water to boil,

waiting for the dentist,

waiting for the bathroom.

I was pretty sure this was all part of their plan. Making me wait was just the beginning. Who knew what Vice Principal Kline and Mrs. Bunker had in store for me! I could just imagine it:

DETENTION
SUSPENSION
EXPULSION

Not to mention what this meant for my

PERMANENT RECORD!

When something goes on your permanent record, it is with you for LIFE. Hence the word

Bold, all caps, TRIPLE underlined. Not only that, everyone would know. My CHILDREN would know. And my children's children. And my children's children's children! What would they think of me?

All I wanted was to eat a good
lunch and figure out my Thing,
and now my life was OVER—
well, it would be as
soon as Mrs. Kline
opened the door.

Waiting outside her office felt like sinking in
quicksand. I knew I was doomed—
it was just a matter of waiting
(and waiting and waiting . . .)
for it to happen.

The longer I waited, the more time I had to think of all the ways this would RUIN my life.

I braced myself for the worst, but then the strangest thing happened. . . .

She brought me back into her office, sighed, and said—

I'm letting you go with a

There will be NO MORE organized food swaps or snack trades.

*DO YOU UNDERSTAND?

We have school lunch rules for a reason. You can't just decide to change the rules.

I nodded because it seemed like the thing I was supposed to do. Then she let me go.

I walked to my next class in a complete and total daze, thinking this must be what it felt like to narrowly escape death.

The next morning, Mrs. Kline gave a school-wide warning during homeroom announcements:

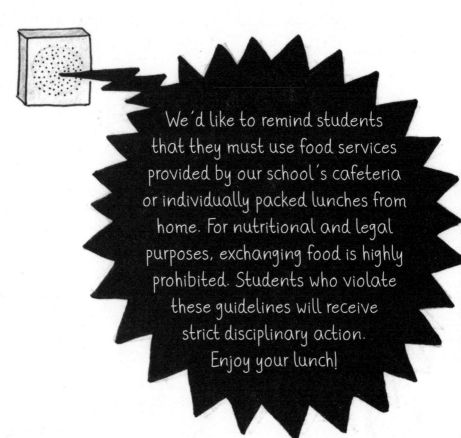

We'd like to remind students that they must use food services provided by our school's cafeteria or individually packed lunches from home. For nutritional and legal purposes, exchanging food is highly prohibited. Students who violate these guidelines will receive strict disciplinary action. Enjoy your lunch!

That's when it hit me.
It was official—
our lunch revolution
was OVER.

Okay, so it could have been worse. I wasn't in (much) trouble and my life wasn't in shambles the way I thought it would be, but this was the end of our lunch exchange and that was pretty sad if you asked me.

For a while, it seemed like things were going well and I was starting to find my place in the Middles. People knew who I was—not for being Peter's sister or for being Maxine and Logan's other friend, but for something I started, something that was MINE.

I should have known it was too good to be true!

At first, everyone seemed just as upset as I was—UNTIL Lana Alvarez spotted a shiny new diamond ring on Miss Myers's finger.

IT WAS HUGE!

Within a matter of hours, the entire school was buzzing.

When would the wedding be?
Was Miss Myers going to change her name??
Which of us would be invited???

Soon our disbanded lunch exchange was old news.

Even Maxine and Logan started moving on.

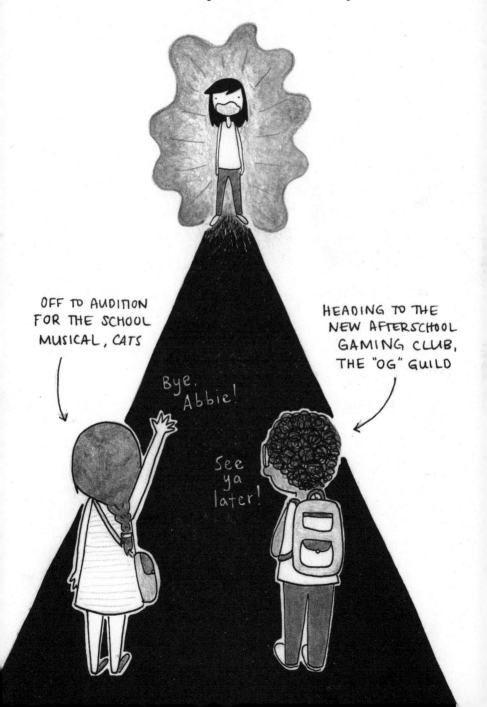

CHAPTER ELEVEN

Our whole operation was ruined. Everything we had been working toward was irrelevant now. It didn't matter. No one even cared. Worst of all, I was still stuck in the Middles and would be for what seemed like FOREVER.

Just thinking about the miserable state of things made me sink into a major funk. It was worse than any other funk I had ever been in—including the time my favorite Saturday-morning cartoon show was canceled.

I wore all black every Saturday for WEEKS.

IT'S OVER! TV WILL NEVER BE THIS GOOD AGAIN!

No, this funk was different. It might've even been contagious, because I noticed Peter started acting weird too.

I thought for a second that maybe my REAL brother had been abducted by aliens or replaced by a cyborg clone or switched with an evil twin. Anything was possible.

Then the weirdest thing happened.

He came to pick me up after school, which made no sense because Peter never EVER picked me up after school. He didn't explain why he was there—all he said was:

Then he yanked my backpack right off my back and started walking. At that point, he had taken my personal property hostage. Even if this person was an alternate, evil version of my brother, I had no choice but to follow him.

In retrospect, this was a good decision because we ended up in front of Antonia's Bake Shop!

Peter offered to buy me a cinnamon sticky bun with extra frosting. He knew I had a weakness for frosting. Was this ANOTHER trap?

I decided to accept the pastry, but I wasn't going to let him off that easy. I had to get some answers.

WHAT'S GOING ON?

why are you here? why am I here?

What is this? what's the catch?

My mouth was still kind of full and crumbs went flying across the table. Peter didn't seem to mind, which was also weird because he usually tells me this makes me look like a caveman.

Instead, he said:

I thought you might be having a **HARD WEEK.**

Want to **TALK** about it?

(He somehow sounded both LIKE Peter and NOT like Peter at the same time.)

I was stuck—I DID and DIDN'T. After all, Peter and I were nothing alike. He made it all the way through the Middles, and at the rate I was going, I would be lucky if I even made it to seventh grade.

HOW COULD HE possibly understand?

But he was my brother and he brought me here and he bought me food, so I didn't have much to lose. I just needed to relate it to something we both understood—

I started to explain.

Just the right amount of sugary sweetness, a balanced frosting-to-dough ratio, and the perfect combination of flavor and texture.

The pastries at Antonia's are the **BEST**.

Everyone knows that—

—but you know who we **NEVER** think of?

The sad little *reject pastry* that gets left in the back of the bakery.

WHAT? HUH?

There's always ONE pastry that's just...

NOT GOOD ENOUGH.

It's lopsided or it doesn't have enough *chocolate* pieces or it's BURNT on the side.

So that pastry gets left out and has to watch all its pastry friends go off in a shiny display case for everyone to see them.

I bet that pastry feels left behind, sitting in the bakery where no one can see it and no one knows that it even ex—

Peter started laughing and said:

UM... so would I be a cupcake in this scenario?!?

HMPH!

"That's not the point! All the sad reject pastry wants is to be with her friends and find her Thing! You just don't get it."

MAYBE NOT...

"But sometimes you won't know for sure if you're doing your Thing.

Sometimes you change.

Or your Thing will change. You might be absolutely sure one minute and then later, you're not.

Don't think about it so much. The truth is, no one really knows for sure. Not even me.

You are not a reject pastry— you're just in middle school. "

Maybe Peter understood me more than I thought. We ended up talking for a long time—so long that Peter got a text from Mom saying that if we didn't get home soon, she wasn't going to let us in for dinner.

where ARE you? If you both aren't home by dinner, I'm NOT saving you ANY... xoxo MOM

Once we left the bakery, I noticed that Peter was carrying ANOTHER pastry. We'd eaten so many already—even I thought this was excessive!

But then—

HERE. This is for you... ... for lunch tomorrow.

Did he know what happened to the lunch exchange? Did he know it was my idea?

Before I got the chance to ask, some members of the high school varsity soccer team spotted us waiting at the bus stop and offered to give us a ride home.

Sometimes being Peter Wu's sister had its perks.

CHAPTER TWELVE

Back at school, the eighth graders continued to rule the cafeteria with an iron fist, and the lunch ladies continued to let them.

I made some formal complaints, but nothing changed.

SCHOOL SUGGESTION BOX

It seemed like now that the lunch exchange had failed, everyone was willing to accept that things were just BAD and there was nothing we could do.

Well, in TWO YEARS, WE'll be in eighth grade.

The only people who still cared about it were the kids in study hall.

Alexis felt bad about ratting me out to her mom, so she offered to share all her class notes with me for a YEAR.

Everyone else was waiting for the next move—for MY next move. What they didn't know was that the lunch exchange had been IT, my one big Thing.

They expected a  but I had NOTHING.

I had used up all my good ideas.

It was only a matter of time before they found out the truth, and I couldn't bring myself to face them, so for the first time, I spent the whole study hall period

ACTUALLY STUDYING.

Definitely a sign that things were off.

The entire Universe must have been out of whack because nothing was going the way it usually did.

For one thing, Aunt Lisa showed up unexpectedly that night. It wasn't the right day for our usual Friday night family dinner, but for some reason, there she was.

Of course, Aunt Lisa probably came over BECAUSE she sensed things were off.

The minute she saw me, she immediately asked what was wrong.

After a little prodding . . .

I cracked
and told her
everything.

Well, it sounds like you tried something out and it just didn't work. That's okay.

Suddenly, she leaned in, and whispered. Then she winked.

not everything has to work out.

What did that mean? What was the point of doing something if you knew it wasn't going to work out? Wasn't the Thing working out the whole point of doing the Thing?

She could probably tell by the look on my face that I wasn't buying it, but all she said was

in a totally vague and cryptic way before disappearing into the backyard.

Probably to commune with nature or something like that.

Maybe Aunt Lisa really is nuts.

In fact, I was starting to think that ALL adults were actually nuts—especially the ones running Pointdexter Middle School.

Even though most of the students had already dismissed the idea of reviving our lunch revolution or staging some kind of cafeteria uprising, the teachers at school just wouldn't let it go!

It's like they were paranoid the school was about to descend into chaos and anarchy!

One warning announcement wasn't enough for them. They had to remind us CONSTANTLY. The number of signs about cafeteria rules and regulations practically tripled overnight! Talk about wasting paper.

Ms. Skelter must have realized that the whole thing started under her watch, and she intended to punish us for it.

One day, instead of letting us work on homework like she usually did, she made us write an essay about the consequences of rule breaking. Then she went off on this long, ranting lecture—

HOLD ON!

NOT FAIR.
I cannot - SILENT
WILL NOT be anymore
I have to say
SOMETHING
- not just for
me, but
for all of
US
1ST
in SCHOOL.
Everything is
Confusing and
different and
just so weird.
BARELY have
place here.
LUNCHTIME
is supposed
to be

...way things are, it doesn't feel like ANYTHING is OURS. sometimes the SCHOOL acts like we aren't important and NO ONE notices but US. IT'S NOT RIGHT. Isn't this OUR SCHOOL too?

WE...what we want! shouldn't we be able to say what WE THINK and how we FEEL? shouldn't we have a VOICE? Don't we have THE RIGHT to be HEARD?

As I stood there in front of everyone, I felt a strange tingling feeling—like a nervous and excited spark.

I had everyone's attention! What I was doing didn't just matter to ME, it mattered to THEM.

We had all been denied access to decent cafeteria food and conned out of our best snacks by eighth graders and unfairly brushed aside by tyrannical lunch ladies. Someone had to say something. . . .

so why NOT me?

I had to say something—not just for me, but for the kids around me in that creaky classroom trailer. For the kids sitting in all the other classrooms around school. For the next generation of kids. For the future!

That's when it crossed my mind . . .

Maybe THIS was my calling. Maybe THIS was my Thing! I was the voice of the people!

THE VOICE OF THE PEOPLE!

I don't know what made me get up from my seat and interrupt Ms. Skelter. I NEVER spoke in class and I definitely never spoke while a teacher was speaking!

Was I changing? Was this even me? I wasn't sure if I was becoming someone new or if I was just now figuring out that this had always been me.

WHO WAS I, REALLY?

Just thinking about it was confusing.

Before I started middle school, I had really just
wanted to make it through without a fuss. I
just wanted to survive.

But there I was, orchestrating lunch revolutions
and getting called to the vice principal's office
and being asked to stay after class.

I waited for Skeletor to unleash her wrath and seal my fate.

She called me Abbie! I thought that was weird because until this point, I wasn't positive she even knew my name.

Here it was—a hex or a curse or, at the very least, detention!

I DO, however, support PASSION. What you said about this school — you're NOT wrong. Pointdexter needs students who care — just maybe in the RIGHT way.

This was NOT the conversation I had expected. I imagined there would be icy glares and voodoo involved. Instead, Ms. Skelter seemed to be acting almost NICE.

She told me I was free to go, but just as I was leaving, she asked . . .

I can't remember my response because I basically blacked out at that moment. I didn't regain my composure or normal mental functions until about twenty minutes into my next class.

When I told Maxine and Logan what happened later, they thought it was the coolest thing EVER.

WOAH! OMG. That's crazy! UNBELIEVABLE.

"So are you going to do it?" Logan asked. "Sixth-grade class president: Abbie Wu?"

It was the craziest idea I'd ever heard. I couldn't even really imagine it. Then again . . .

GO TEAM WU!

VOTE WU

VOTE ABBIE WU FOR CLASS PRESIDENT

WU

VOTE FOR WHO? ABBIE WU

ABBIE for PRESIDENT

ABBIE WU! SHE'LL WORK FOR YOU!

Who knew? I probably wasn't meant to be the spokesperson for my generation just yet, but maybe I would be—someday.

Or maybe I could be something else entirely.

When we put our heads together and thought about it, there were a lot of possibilities.

After a while, we ended up imagining a future with transportation pods, teacher holograms, and robot dogs.

That sounded way more fun anyway.

I don't know, though. Maybe Peter is right and it isn't about finding

Maybe it's more about just doing something that you care about and just doing THINGS—plural.

"Well? What do you think?" Maxine asked.

Despite what Aunt Lisa says, I know I will never be good at meditating. I am, however, trying to think LESS and let things figure themselves out MORE.

So I just shrugged. *We'll see.*

That's the thing about the Middles. They're complicated and things inside them are always changing. So for now, it's enough just knowing I have a chance and thinking . . .

maybe I'm NOT 100% DOOMED.

ACKNOWLEDGMENTS

Finding the words to thank everyone who helped make this book a BOOK is impossibly hard. All my gratitude, appreciation, and FEELINGS cannot possibly be contained on just these pages. But I have to try, so here goes:

Margaret Anastas, there is no *Frazzled* without you. You always understand what I want to say and help me find the best ways to say it. I am so lucky to have an editor who is as encouraging, kind, and hilarious as you . . . not to mention one who genuinely seems to think *I* am hilarious too.

Cindy Hamilton, you are the best of the best, the definition of a gladiator. There is no way to possibly measure what you've done for me and Abbie Wu. You are our greatest champion and deserve all the good things *ever*.

Steve Malk. I don't know exactly where I'd be without you, but I definitely wouldn't be *here*. Thank you for rooting for me from the start and for helping me find my own voice. There is no one I'd rather have on my side than you. Thank you also to my Writers House people, especially Hannah Mann and the incomparable Michael Mejias. You told me to "use my words," and look, I did! Sort of—there are pictures too.

This book would not exist without the amazing efforts of everyone at HarperCollins Children's Books. I couldn't have asked for a better home for *Frazzled*. It really feels like I'm with family, and I don't think it can get much better than that.

To Suzanne, Susan, Kate, and Emily, thank you for seeing something in me and placing so much faith in a book of doodles and an unknown debut. To Barb, Amy, Whitney, and the designers who helped me figure out how to make a book, thank you for using your killer design skills to make me look good. To all my copyeditors, you are lovely people for working on this crazy project and watching my back so closely.

Thank you to Andrea, Kathy, Kerry, and the amazing sales team for carrying this book to a level of excitement that I could never have imagined. Thank you to every member of marketing who worked on this book, particularly Team Middle Grade and brilliant masterminds Kim and Matt. I knew things would be good if you geniuses were behind it. Thank you also to the Sweet Suite (past generations and honorary members included) for appreciating all the weird things I say and always supporting #frazzled. To Jonathan, Alison, and Alia, a million hugs for always listening.

Thanks to Aubry for setting this crazy thing into motion and Lindsey for bringing up doodling at dinner that one time. To the publicity team, for always making it fun no matter what. You constantly impress me with what you do, and I wish I could give you all private islands. Can't wait for our amazing bed-and-breakfast! And to Caroline, who is impossibly cool and infinitely wise, thank you for your guidance this past year. I would follow you off a cliff.

Thank you to my whole family, but especially to you, Mom, for raising me to pursue the things I love and actually trusting in the validity of that pursuit. And to Chucaloo, for keeping me sane throughout this whole process—or at least making me feel like it was all going to be okay even if I was a little crazy.

I wish I could name all the people who have encouraged and supported me up to this point. The list is very, very long. I don't know how I managed to befriend such amazingly wonderful people, but trust me when I say that I appreciate you ALL. Especially Flawless, for giving me the kind of friendships I can always count on.

So much of who I was when I was a kid and who I am now is written into the pages of this book, so my last bit of thanks is to my readers, whoever and wherever you are. This thing is as much yours as it is mine. Thank you for taking the time to live a little in Abbie's head and for giving her a little space in yours.

Kamoplat Trangratapit

BOOKI VIVAT has been doodling somewhat seriously since 2011 and not-so-seriously since childhood. She grew up in Southern California and graduated from the University of California, San Diego. She currently works in publishing and lives in Brooklyn, New York. This is her first novel. You can follow her on Instagram at @bookibookibooki and on Twitter at @thebookiv.